For Constantin and Alexandra
J. W.
For Molly
C. S.

Creative Editions is an imprint of The Creative Company, 123 South
Broad Street, Mankato, Minnesota 56001.

Library of Congress Cataloging-in-Publication Data

Wahl, Jan.
I met a dinosaur/by Jan Wahl; illustrated by Chris Sheban.
p. cm.
"Creative Editions."
Summary: After a visit to a museum of natural history, a young girl
begins to see dinosaurs everywhere.
ISBN 0-15-201644-9
[1. Dinosaurs—Fiction. 2. Imagination—Fiction. 3. Stories in rhyme.] I.
Sheban, Chris, ill. II. Title.
PZ8.3.W133Iae 1997   [E]—dc21   96-44583

First edition

A C E F D B

Printed in Italy

I MET A DINOSAUR

By

JAN WAHL

Illustrated by

CHRIS SHEBAN

CREATIVE EDITIONS

Mankato

HARCOURT BRACE & COMPANY

San Diego New York London

I

MET A

DINOSAUR

AND A

DINOSAUR

MET ME

AT THE MUSEUM

OF NATURAL

HISTORY.

"GIRL,

IT'S JUST BONES."

GRAY BONES,

THEY SAY.

THIS WASN'T TRUE

FOR ME

WHEN WE

LEFT THAT

DAY.

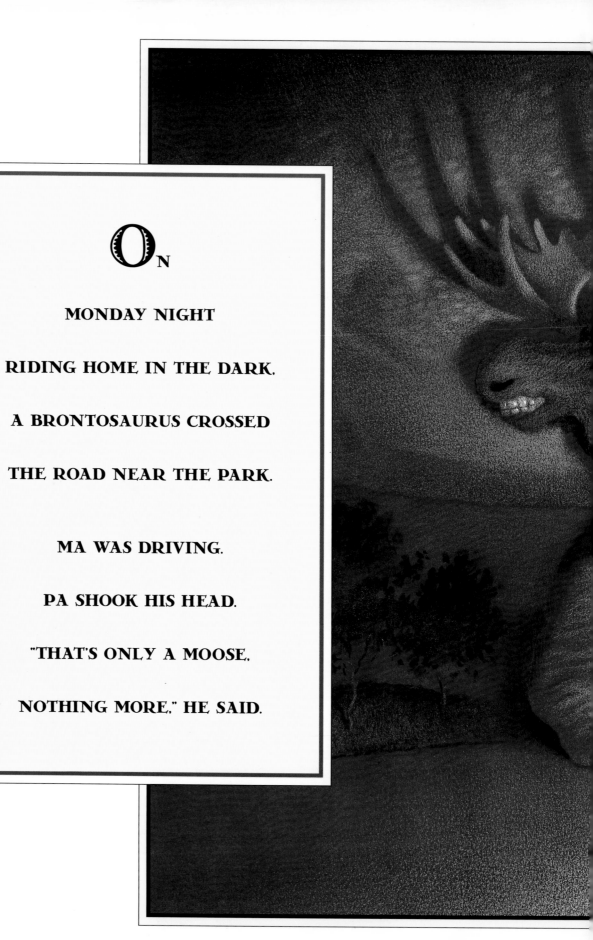

On

MONDAY NIGHT

RIDING HOME IN THE DARK,

A BRONTOSAURUS CROSSED

THE ROAD NEAR THE PARK.

MA WAS DRIVING.

PA SHOOK HIS HEAD.

"THAT'S ONLY A MOOSE,

NOTHING MORE," HE SAID.

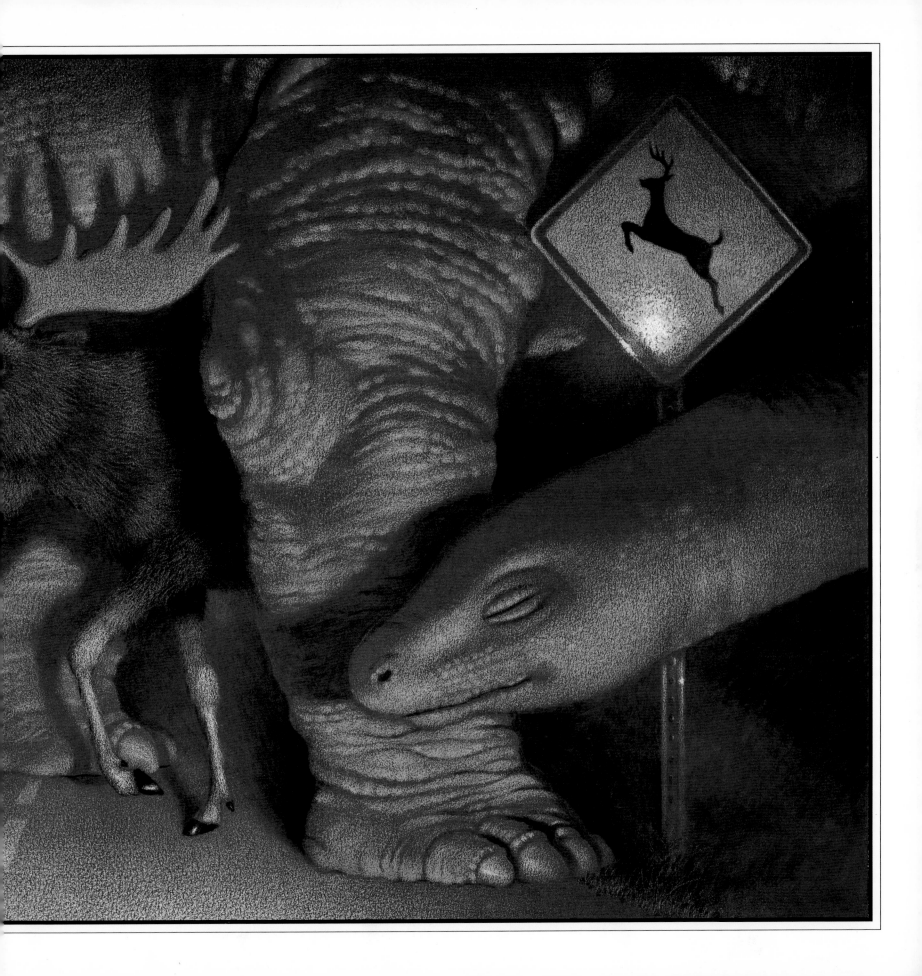

EAR

OUR HOUSE,

ABOUT A BLOCK AWAY,

ON TUESDAY I SAW

A STEGOSAURUS AT PLAY.

SHE WAS AT THE GAS STATION

AMID PUMPS, CARS AND MORE

ROLLING HER EYES

BY THE STATION'S FRONT DOOR.

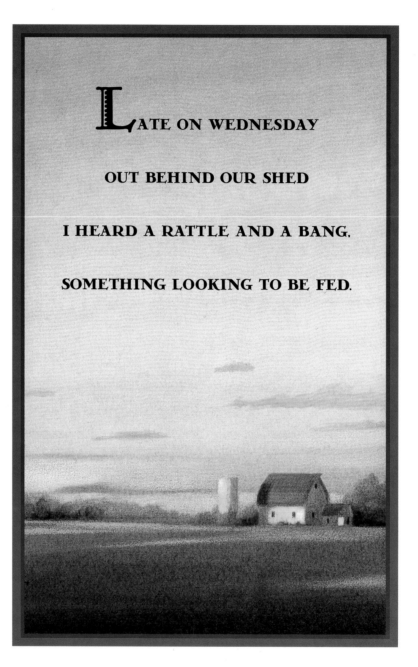

LATE ON WEDNESDAY

OUT BEHIND OUR SHED

I HEARD A RATTLE AND A BANG,

SOMETHING LOOKING TO BE FED.

"A TINY DIMETRODON," I SANG

AS I STARED THROUGH THE GLASS.

"JUST A RACCOON," CALLED PA.

"OR A COW EATING GRASS."

AT

THE EDGE OF TOWN

NEAR THE RAILROAD TRACK

STAND TWO ELECTRIC TOWERS,

LIGHTS SHINING IN THE BLACK.

ON THURSDAY

I SAW A BLINK FROM THE TOWERS.

HELLO, TRICERATOPS.

I STOOD THERE FOR HOURS.

On

FRIDAY PA AND I

ROWED FAR OUT ON THE LAKE.

IT STARTED TO RAIN.

I SAW SOMETHING GIVE A SHAKE.

PA LET OUT A SIGH.

"A LOG THAT SOMETHING'S SITTING ON."

"NO, NO!" I CRIED.

"IT LOOKS LIKE AN IGUANODON."

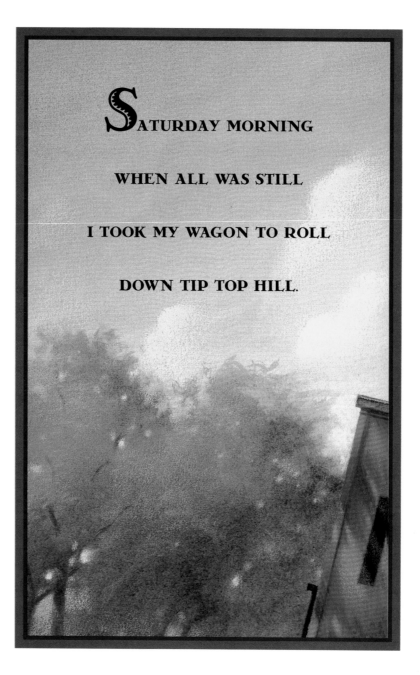

SATURDAY MORNING

WHEN ALL WAS STILL

I TOOK MY WAGON TO ROLL

DOWN TIP TOP HILL.

LOOKING DOWN FROM THE HEIGHT

I GOT A PUSH FROM THE BREEZE.

THAT WAS NO MOVING VAN

BY THE BUTTONWOOD TREES.

T
Y
R
A
N
N
O
S
A
U
R
U
S

A

TYRANNOSAURUS

PEERED PAST

A LEAFY LIMB.

WITH HIS SHORT

ARM, HE WAVED.

I WAVED

BACK AT

HIM.

Sunday

AFTERNOON WAS PERFECT

TO FLY MY KITE.

HIGH UP IT FLEW!

THE STRING PULLED TIGHT.

I SQUINTED MY EYE.

I COULD SEE IT JUST FINE.

A PTERODACTYL PULLED

ON THE END OF THE LINE.

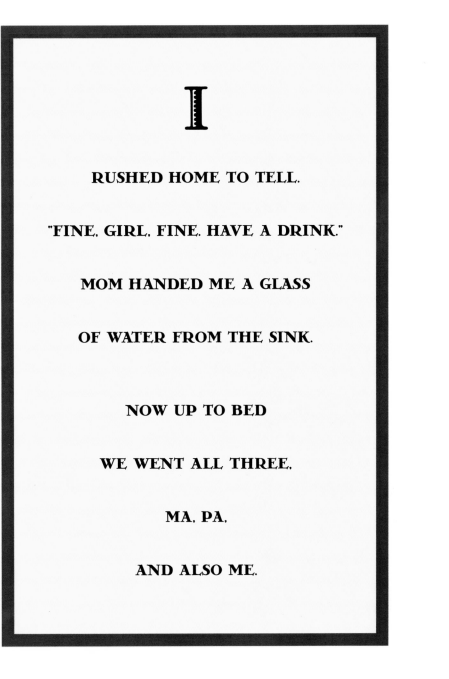

I

RUSHED HOME TO TELL.

"FINE. GIRL. FINE. HAVE A DRINK."

MOM HANDED ME A GLASS

OF WATER FROM THE SINK.

NOW UP TO BED

WE WENT ALL THREE,

MA. PA,

AND ALSO ME.

"**L**IGHTS OFF!

STOP READING.

IT'S TIME FOR BED.

CLOSE YOUR EYES, GIRL,

LAY DOWN YOUR HEAD."

I STAYED QUITE STILL,

I TURNED MY THOUGHTS DOWN.

OUTSIDE THE WINDOW, A FOG

CREPT ROUND THE TOWN.

D
I
N
O
S
A
U
R
S

EFORE

I SLEEP,

I CAN'T COUNT

SHEEP.

I SEE DINOSAURS

EVERYWHERE.

COULD BE ONE

SITTING IN MY

CHAIR.

Dinosaurs and other creatures

(in Order of Appearance)

TRICERATOPS. "three-horned face," had a huge head, seven feet long. It had one stubby horn on its nose and two horns above its eyes. Weighing five tons, it survived on the plants of the forest. It was one of the last dinosaurs on earth.

ALLOSAURUS. "different lizard," was one of the largest dinosaurs in North America—thirty-five feet long from head to tail. On its hind legs, it stood fifteen feet tall. It was a meat-eater and a very powerful animal with strong leg muscles and sharp claws on its front feet.

BRONTOSAURUS. "thunder lizard," lived near rivers, browsing on treetops and ferns. A solid animal with an extremely long neck and an even longer tail, it measured seventy feet. It weighed over twenty-four tons, the equivalent of five elephants. When its fossils were found to match another dinosaur, its name was corrected to Apatosaurus.

STEGOSAURUS. "roof lizard," had a small head, a back ridged with plates and a spiky tail. About the length of a big truck, it grazed the plains and could defend itself by swinging its dangerous tail.

DIMETRODON. "two sizes of teeth," was a four-legged, meat-eating reptile that lived before the dinosaurs. Besides having two different kinds of teeth (actually it had three), it's known for the webbed sail on its back. The sail helped Dimetrodon control its body temperature. By turning the sail to catch the sun's rays, it could warm up.

IGUANODON. "iguana tooth," walked on its back feet, using its front feet to pull down leaves to eat. It might have defended itself by sticking its spiky thumb into its enemy. This five-ton dinosaur, twenty-five feet long, traveled in herds.

TYRANNOSAURUS. "tyrant lizard," one of the largest meat-eating dinosaurs, ran on its two hind legs. From nose to tail, it was fifty feet long and had huge saw like teeth that were up to seven inches long. Unlike many dinosaurs, it had eyes that faced forward, allowing it to judge distances.

PTERODACTYLS. "wing fingers," were a group of flying reptiles, with wing spans ranging from that of a sparrow to that of a small airplane. They ate insects and fish and used the wind to soar with their featherless wings.

DROMICEIOMIMUS. "emu mimic," was as big as an ostrich or emu and looked like one too. It lived in the forest of western Canada and preyed on small animals. It could run more than fifty miles per hour.

DIPLODOCUS. "double beam," was one of the longest dinosaurs, measuring ninety feet—head to tail. It might have been semiaquatic, living on water plants. It had a barrel-shaped body, stubby legs, a long neck and tail, and a tiny head.